(Un)lucky Thirteen

Suzi Wieland

Twisted Path Press

Chapter One

Cara figured she'd have to marry well.

The house she was standing in front of, her dream house and a work of art, was a pale green Victorian home on the corner of Twenty-Sixth Street and Thirteenth Avenue. Unfortunately, she would never afford a home like this on her salary.

It was three stories, had large windows, and had a small turret on one corner that Cara was dying to see the inside of. Having a bedroom there would be like living in a castle. The house had weathered the last century so gracefully, unlike a few of the other homes in the neighborhood, including Cara's own tiny house.

She imagined sitting on that swing on the porch, a book in one hand and a glass of wine in the other as she took shade from the hot summers. Someday Cara would have such a home.

I'd better get going. The homeowners might spy her through the window and call the cops.

(UN)LUCKY THIRTEEN

She continued down the sidewalk and took in the small one-car garage hiding behind the house and the white picket fence surrounding the yard. A black tire hung lazily from one of the large oak trees on one side, and on the other was a garden full of all sorts of vegetables. They even had a sandbox and a gazebo shrouded in greenery and speckled with delicate purple flowers.

"Hello," a voice chirped, and Cara startled. She peered down at the little sweetheart behind the fence with her curly sun-kissed blonde hair held back by a wide pink check headband that matched her frilly dress. Her bright blue eyes sparkled with mischief, and Cara guessed she was around five. Cara's niece Mattie was four and seemed about the same age.

"Oh, hi. I didn't see you there." Cara swiped her long black hair behind her ears to stop the breeze from blowing it in her face. She should've put her hair in a ponytail.

"My name's Lindsey. And this is my house." She waved as if showcasing it.

"I'm Cara. Nice to meet you. I hope you don't mind I was admiring your home."

Lindsey shook her head. Those pale cheeks with just a hint of color—they were so pinchable. "It's been in the family for generations."

A laugh rumbled in Cara's chest. Lindsey must've heard those words often from her parents or grandparents. A wave of longing swept through Cara. She was only two hours away from her parents and a bunch of nieces and nephews, but getting home to see them was so hard.

"Well, you are very lucky to have such a stunning home."

"Yes, it is magnificent. Would you like to see the inside?"

The answer was a big yes, but Cara couldn't exactly follow this little girl inside. Her parents would freak out. At least Cara would if she had a kid who brought a perfect stranger into the house.

"Lindsey," a man called from the back porch. He looked around the backyard, and his eyes popped open when he saw Cara. He stuck his hands in the pockets of his shorts and stood there stiffly.

"I was talking to my new friend, Cara. Isn't she pretty?"

Cara's cheeks burned pink. "Aren't you sweet."

"I need a new mommy. Mine is gone." The angelic face smiled so warmly that Cara wondered if Lindsey was about to try set her up with her dad. Was he divorced, or was her mother dead?

"Um, Lindsey." Her father ran a hand through his shaggy dark brown hair. "When do you want to eat?"

"In a bit. I want to give Cara a tour of the house first. I'm showing her my room and my doll." Lindsey squared her shoulders and crossed her arms, staring off at her father, but he didn't answer. The silence grew awkward, the father not agreeing but not disagreeing, and Lindsey not backing down.

Cara checked her phone. "Oh, I'm sorry, Lindsey. I really would like that tour, but I'm meeting a friend in twenty minutes."

"You have time." Her blue eyes grew wide, tugging at Cara's sensibilities. The good-looking father was also an enticing factor, and she guessed he was close to her age, but she just couldn't stay.

"I don't. I'm sorry. I have a ten-minute walk home, and I might be late as it is."

Lindsey's lip stuck out. "Do you promise to come back and see me again? I want to show you my house. You'll love it."

"I promise. I'd love to see the rest of your yard too." A stone path started under a flowered trellis and led through the yard, but the trees at the very back were too thick for Cara to see through.

"Deal." Lindsey stuck her delicate hand out to shake. Her tiny painted fingernails matched her toenails, a smooth paint job that Cara figured Lindsey's father had done— what a good man.

"Deal." Cara shook hands with her and took off down the sidewalk.

"Don't forget you promised," Lindsey sang in a sweet voice, and Cara chuckled.

"I know."

The little girl disappeared, and Cara snuck one last peek at the house. Lindsey's father was standing on the back steps, head turned in her direction. A small shiver rolled through her at his intense stare, and she gave him a little wave.

Chapter Two

Almost a week passed before Cara was able to go for a longer walk. Her boss in her HR department had strongly encouraged her to stay late when overtime was needed, and she was exhausted in the evenings when she got home. She wanted to move up in the company, and working those hours when her co-workers refused might give her a leg up.

She approached the Victorian home and glanced up at the front door. Lindsey might not remember Cara, and her father might not even allow a tour, but she sure hoped so.

When she passed by the house, nobody was in the backyard.

The third day she got over there, she walked around the house to the sidewalk next to the backyard. Lindsey's father was on his knees in the garden, a pile of weeds next to him. He was cute with his dark brown hair and five-o'clock shadow, and his face glistened as he tugged weeds out. It was sexy, seeing a man working hard.

Cara stepped up to the white picket fence and inhaled the fresh scent of cut grass. Their yard was immaculate.

"That doesn't look like too much fun."

He looked up in surprise and then glanced at the house. "Oh, not really, but Lindsey loves fresh vegetables. The peas came in well this summer."

"A child who likes vegetables?" Cara laughed. "That's rare." Most of her nieces and nephews were fairly picky, except for maybe one.

"Lindsey's not like other girls her age." He frowned and stared off toward the house again. Something fluttered in the window—a curtain maybe. He cleared his throat. "Lindsey's a special girl."

"I bet every father says that." Cara's father had. Of course, she was the fifth and final child after four boys, and her dad always loved his little girl. "I'm Cara, by the way."

"Uh, Kyle." He stood and offered a dirt-covered hand.

She looked down, and he jerked his hand back. "Sorry. Wasn't paying attention."

"How old is Lindsey?" Cara shielded her eyes. The hot sun bore down on her, and she wished for the clouds to slide over and block off the harsh rays.

He hesitated for a moment. "She's five."

"And is she your only child?"

"Yes." Kyle toed at the ground with a dirty shoe. "My only. She's been talking about you non-stop. She doesn't have many friends in the neighborhood."

"Lindsey seems like a sweet girl." She debated her next question but figured she had to ask. "So is it just you two in that big house?"

Cara's house growing up had been half the size, but being the only girl, she lucked out and got her own bedroom. With four brothers though, noise always filled their home. She'd lived there all through college and a few years after. She didn't leave until recently when she'd gotten her new job and moved a few hours away, and sometimes she missed the chaos. Somebody was always hanging around the house.

"Yes. Her mom died years ago." He shrugged.

"I'm sorry." Cara didn't know what to say. He didn't seem all that broken up about it, but he probably hid his grief. "And I don't want you to worry. I know it'd be weird for Lindsey to bring me into your home when we've just met. So I won't hold her to her promise."

"There's nothing special inside," Kyle whispered. "Actually, we're doing renovations, so it might not be the best time for visitors. There's a big mess inside, everything all over the place. Lots of tools and other things you might trip over and all."

"Oh, okay." She got the feeling he didn't really want her to come in, but she couldn't blame him. He didn't know her at all.

"I'd better get inside though." Kyle quickly stuffed the weeds into a plastic bag. "I, um… I'll tell her you stopped by. She'll understand though. The house is such a mess."

He stood just as the door opened. The doorway framed the little girl, her hands on her hips. Kyle took off for the back porch, leaving the weeds in the garden.

Lindsey waved at Cara excitedly and met Kyle at the steps. He spoke to her in a quiet voice, and the smile fell from her face. She eyed Cara as Kyle rushed back and snatched his bag of weeds.

"She's not feeling well. She hasn't been for a while. She probably shouldn't have any visitors until she's better." He backed away from Cara.

Okay. That's weird. He definitely didn't want her around here.

Cara ignored Kyle and waved to Lindsey, then set off down the sidewalk.

She took a peek back before she hit the garage. Kyle seemed to be arguing with Lindsey, but Cara couldn't hear what they were saying.

This was a total bummer. Kyle had seemed normal at first, but he obviously had some issues. Lindsey didn't look sick, and she'd seemed to want to see Cara, but that wouldn't happen.

Kyle's behavior made her even more curious about him and his daughter. Cara shouldn't come back, but she knew she would. Just to check on things.

(UN)LUCKY THIRTEEN

The big cloud finally covered the sun, giving Cara some welcome relief. If Kyle didn't want her to visit Lindsey, she couldn't exactly go against his wishes, but she wanted to make sure Lindsey was okay, that it wasn't something serious.

She'd stop back one more time, and then she'd leave them alone.

Chapter Three

On her next walk a few weeks later, Cara passed by the house again, hoping to see Lindsey.

"Cara!" Lindsey squealed when she came around the garage. The adorable white sailor dress with blue and red stripes bounced up and down as Lindsey clapped her hands. "I've been waiting for you to come back."

"Are you okay? Kyle—your daddy said you weren't feeling well the other day."

"Yes, I'm fine and dandy. But I missed you. That's why I was sick."

Cara chuckled at her fancy words. Children were so melodramatic.

"But you're all better now." Cara glanced up to check if Kyle was around but didn't see him.

"Yes." She nodded her head triumphantly. "Now are you ready to tour the house?"

"Oh, your dad said now isn't a good time. With the renovations and all."

Lindsey put her hands on her hips and laughed. "Daddy was being silly. The house was messy, and he was embarrassed."

He'd seemed more reluctant than that.

"I help him clean sometimes, but I don't do a good job." Lindsey lowered her head and frowned. "I try."

"I bet you do." She's only five after all.

Lindsey brightened. "But Daddy said it's okay now. You wanted to see the garden, didn't you? Come on in." Lindsey waved at Cara and ran toward the trellis.

Cara hesitated, not sure Kyle would approve, but Lindsey had said he said it was okay, so she stepped through the gate and closed it behind her. She took a deep breath of the fragrant honeysuckle on the trellis.

"This is gorgeous." Cara fingered the vines entwined over the trellis and eyed the large oaks. Her own backyard only had a few trees, nothing to this extent.

"Follow the yellow brick road." Lindsey grinned and stood on the stone path. She giggled and reached out for Cara's hand. "And don't worry. I won't let you get lost."

"Oh, thank you. I was a little worried about disappearing in such a big yard, so I'm glad you're here with me." She played up her concerns, hoping Lindsey would think she meant it. That would make Lindsey feel important.

"Do you want to tell your dad we're going back here?" She still hadn't caught sight of Kyle.

"No, we're fine. He knows you're here."

They stepped hand-in-hand through the arch. The canopy of trees provided a cool relief from the heat, and as they walked, Lindsey pointed out another flower garden, her favorite water fountain, which had water running down a rock wall, and her bird bath.

"Well, it's not my bird bath. It's for all my birdy friends who come to visit."

"Do they have names?" Cara asked.

"Of course. Virginia and Beatrice and Pearl and Alma. And Stanley and Eugene too."

Cara stifled a laugh. Unusual choices from a little girl today. Maybe they were some distant relatives of hers.

"Those are beautiful names."

"And look at this." Lindsey ran to the corner and plopped down in front of a tree stump. "This is my fairy home. Isn't it neat?"

"That's awesome." A steep roof covered the three-foot-high stump, and four window frames and a door were stuck to the front side. A river of blue glass rock flowed alongside the tree, and flowers surrounded the stump. Lindsey had little fairies placed around. Cara knelt down next to Lindsey, the soft grass tickling her legs.

"Wow. I wish I had something like this growing up." She'd had plenty of dolls and other girly toys, but somehow she'd ended up playing with her brothers' toys a lot too.

(UN)LUCKY THIRTEEN

"This is Helen, Florence, and Rose." Lindsey pointed to the fairy statuettes. "They keep the bad people out of my garden. And bugs too." Lindsey wrinkled up her nose.

"Good. I don't like bugs either." Cara laughed.

Lindsey entertained Cara with fairy stories over the next half hour. She had the same imagination that Cara's little nieces and nephews had.

Cara wiped her forehead and leaned back on her hands. Even in the shade, it was hot.

"Lemonade. We need lemonade." Lindsey jumped to her feet and tugged on Cara's hand. "Let's go."

"I'm coming." Cara smiled. "You know my niece Mattie loves lemonade too. Her favorite is pink lemonade. What's yours?"

"Lavender-thyme is my favorite."

Okay, that's unusual. Cara wasn't even sure she'd ever heard of that flavor.

"Does your daddy make that for you?" she asked.

"No, one of my mommies did."

Cara came to an abrupt stop. "What do you mean one of your mommies?"

"A grandma is like a mommy." Lindsey gazed up at Cara with her big blue eyes and led them past the tire swing and to the back porch. "You wait here." She disappeared into the house and a few minutes later came out with two glasses full of lemonade and ice. She sat next to Cara on the swing and handed a glass over.

Cara held the sweating glass to her cheek before taking a drink. "This is the best lemonade ever." And she wasn't exaggerating.

Lindsey's chin jutted out, and her head tilted to the side. "It's made from scratch. Daddy does it for me because I don't like the powdered stuff."

"I'm not sure I've ever had lemonade from scratch. It's definitely better."

"It's heavenly," Lindsey agreed, and Cara almost laughed. She had to tell her sister-in-law Riya about Lindsey's extensive vocabulary.

They sat quietly for a few moments, and Cara relished the cold, sweet drink.

"Cara," Lindsey said quietly. "Will you be my momma?" Her sad eyes reflected a pain Cara had not yet seen. It must be so hard to grow up without a mother, to miss out on things like playing dress up and singing songs or sitting with her as she braided your hair.

"I can't just be your mommy. In order for that to happen, me and your daddy would have to fall in love."

"Then fall in love." She said it so seriously, like falling in love was the same as picking up the phone and ordering a pizza.

"You're such a sweetheart. I'd love to be your mommy, but I don't love your daddy. We don't even know each other."

"But you will."

"Yes, we can get to know each other, but it's not guaranteed that we'll fall in love."

"But you'll try?" Her voice held so much hope.

Oh, this girl was killing her. Cara couldn't break her heart and say no, and who knew what would happen. Kyle was a good-looking guy, and she was open to getting to know him better, but maybe he wasn't ready to date yet.

Besides, he wasn't interested in her. He'd practically blown her off that last time she'd been here.

"I'll try." Cara squeezed Lindsey's hand. The little girl smiled, and it warmed Cara's heart. She probably shouldn't have told Lindsey that she'd try, but she didn't want to see the cutie disappointed. Her father could deal with that.

"Let's go in for that tour now." Lindsey stood, pulling Cara to her feet, and they walked through the door into the house.

Cara took in the stunning kitchen: marble countertops, fancy chrome appliances, rich dark cupboards, and drawers galore. "Look at that. Your stove has five burners."

"And two ovens," Lindsey answered. "I want my mommy to have the best kitchen."

A massive fridge stood against the wall surrounded by other shiny silver appliances, and smack dab in the middle of the kitchen was a giant granite island with four barstools.

Lindsey looked at her with wide, curious eyes. "Do you like it?"

"It's a fantastic kitchen. I'm impressed."

"Thank you. I spent months planning it out." Lindsey grinned, and Cara laughed, patting the cute girl on the head. She was getting used to Lindsey's silliness. Maybe she liked to pretend to be an adult like her dad.

"Well, you did a spectacular job." Cara looked across the room to the dining area with its eight-seater table. "And I love that table." The whole living room and dining/kitchen area was open wide. Somebody must've taken out the walls because houses like this were usually very boxy. Cara's sure was.

Bright light spilled from the many windows overlooking the front porch. A beige curved sofa, a leather chair, and a rocking chair surrounded a round ottoman, all sitting in front of a fireplace framed by brown and white speckled marble and topped by an ornately carved mantel. A large TV hung in the space above.

Cara ran her hand over the fuzzy blanket draped over the couch. She could imagine cuddling up here on a cold winter day watching movies.

"Do you like it?" Lindsey asked.

"Very much." She crossed the room and peered through a doorway. "Is that a library?" she said excitedly. She stepped inside before Lindsey had a chance to respond and took in the rich dark woodwork, soft beige walls, and leather loveseat. Even the crown moldings were continued in this room.

(UN)LUCKY THIRTEEN

A computer sat on the desk, and books filled two walls of shelves, and there was a second fireplace. Cara pushed a ladder reaching the highest parts of the dark wood of the shelves of novels. "But I don't see any of your books."

She recognized a lot of classics in the mix, but not one picture book was in the room.

"These are all mine. I've read them all." Lindsey grinned.

Cara sighed. Obviously Lindsey hadn't read any of them. Maybe Kyle had read some to her, but what child would enjoy Quixote or Tolstoy? She didn't see many that were suitable for children.

"I bet you've read them all twice."

"Yes. Now come check out the parlor." Lindsey left the room and crossed over into a short hallway past the steps.

Cara had stepped back in time. A gaudy peach leafy patterned wallpaper covered the walls, topped off by a border of blues and peach and pink. The trim in the room was the same dark color as the library, but vintage lace cream panels blanketed the window, and a grand piano sat in the corner with an antiquish brass lamp next to it.

Lindsey rounded the piano and shook Kyle's arm as he lay snoozing on a beautiful old-style chaise lounge with brass trim and Queen Anne legs. Cara hadn't even noticed him until then.

Two wing-back chairs with the same burgundy velvet and matching side table sat in front of more floor-to-ceiling bookshelves.

"Daddy, Cara's here. Why don't you welcome her home?"

Kyle's eyes flung open, and he jumped off his seat. "Cara!" He blinked quickly and stared at her. Cara's face burned. This wasn't exactly how she'd wanted to see him again.

"Daddy," Lindsey said, a low warning in her voice.

He forced an awkward smile. "It's great to see you. I'm glad you stopped by. When did you get here?"

Hadn't Lindsey said he knew she was there when they were outside?

"Just a bit ago. I was admiring all the work you've done. This home is amazing."

"Thank you," he said, with nothing more. He wasn't the chattiest man around, but she shouldn't blame him. She just popped right in, and she wasn't even sure he wanted her here.

Cara strolled over to the shiny black full-sized grand piano. It struck her then how this house did not seem like that of one with a five-year-old. Three of her brothers had kids, and although their houses were in different states of messiness, even Ty's house, the one where they were the strictest, had fingerprints on the kitchen appliances and random toys sometimes left around. She hadn't seen one toy yet though.

"Do you play the piano?" she asked Kyle.

"I'm learning. But Lindsey's the pianist in the house." He smiled weakly.

"Do you want me to play a song?" Lindsey fluttered her blonde lashes at Cara.

"Of course. Do you know *Mary has a Little Lamb?*"

Lindsey scoffed. "I learned that when I was three." She strutted over to the piano bench, poised her hands above the keys, and closed her eyes.

Her delicate fingers danced across the keys with the ability of a professional. It shouldn't be possible. Cara remembered back to her seven years of piano lessons. The teacher wouldn't let her start until she was six years old because most children that age didn't have the dexterity.

But here was Lindsey playing so gracefully, with so much emotion, a tune Cara recognized couldn't name. The song ended, silence filled the room, and Cara clapped loudly.

"That was amazing. What was it?"

"*Hungarian Dance No. 5* by Brahms. He's one of my favorites."

Kyle remained on the sofa looking out the window at something, acting like his daughter wasn't a child prodigy.

"I'm stunned. I've never heard someone your age play so well."

Lindsey climbed off the piano bench and offered a small curtsey. "Do you play, Cara?"

"I'm afraid not anymore. I took lessons when I was younger, but I quit not long after I started middle school band."

"It's never too late to learn. Daddy is. And you can too. I'll give you lessons."

Okay. Being a prodigy was one thing, but she couldn't be teaching her own father.

"Maybe someday." That probably wouldn't happen, but she didn't need to tell Lindsey that now. As much as Cara loved piano music, it's not like she could play at home. She had no piano and couldn't afford to buy one anytime soon.

She turned to one of the walls, the one covered with gilded frames. Pictures of beautiful women over the ages centered around one large black and white photograph in the middle. A little girl of about Lindsey's age sitting cross-legged in her white dress on a stool. Her expression was somber, but the twinkle in her eye showed a spunk that was being tempered for the photo.

Each photograph featured a different woman truly showcasing the eras. A flapper dress from the twenties. A poodle skirt and cardigan with a string of pearls on the woman's neck from the fifties. Bellbottoms and flashy patterns from the seventies. A power suit with much-too-large shoulder pads from the eighties.

(UN)LUCKY THIRTEEN

Each woman stared grimly at the camera, some in full color, some in black and white. Twelve in all, with the chunky cheeked child in the center.

"Are these the women from your family?" Cara asked in awe of the history adorning the wall.

"They are all the special ladies in my life." Lindsey smiled.

"Can you tell me who they all are?"

"Of course."

Cara listened as Lindsey gave the name of each woman. "And who is the beautiful girl in the middle?" Cara asked.

The pictured girl had a shoulder-length bob and wore a white dress similar to clothing in the early 1900s, but otherwise looked eerily similar to Lindsey.

"That is me, silly." Lindsey gave her a cheeky smile.

Okay then.

"And it looks like you." Cara turned to Kyle. "Is this your side of the family or your wife's?"

"It's my side." Lindsey laughed, and Cara opened her mouth to ask the question again, but Lindsey tugged on her hand and pulled her away from the room. "Let's go show you my room."

The grandfather clock they passed read a quarter after five. "I'll have to be going soon after that," she told Lindsey.

"But you're staying for dinner." Lindsey stopped and pouted at the bottom of the step. "Daddy, tell her she's staying."

"You're welcome to stay," Kyle said.

"Oh, I don't know. I have a lot of things to do." She didn't have much actually but couldn't impose. Lindsey trying to set her up with her father was cute and all, but she didn't want to annoy Kyle. He was friendlier today, but she couldn't get over how he'd acted that one day.

"Of course she will. Daddy is going to make us a nice dinner. He always does what I ask." Lindsey grabbed Cara's arm and snuggled up next to her, blinking those adorable blue eyes. It was the same look Mattie gave her when she was trying to sucker Cara into something too.

"She'd really love for you to stay," Kyle said. "I'll go get dinner ready."

Cara took one more look at the begging girl. "Okay then, you talked me into it."

"I knew you would." Lindsey grinned triumphantly.

Lindsey escorted Cara upstairs, and she admired how the stairway was the centerpiece of the living room on the main floor. Her fingers trailed up the smooth wood bannister topping the ornately carved spindles. It was a work of art in itself.

Upstairs she found a hallway that went both left and right.

"Which way do we go?" she asked.

"This way." Lindsey pointed to the right. "I want to show you my room last."

They strolled down the narrow hallway hand-in-hand, and Lindsey showcased the rooms they passed, including the turret room. They hit the end of the hallway where there was a much smaller staircase to the third floor and had to double back around the U to get to the other side. Cara had expected more modernity, but each room seemed like it had been decorated decades ago and never been updated. None of the rooms held much more than the furniture and a few other small items, and they felt fairly cold and impersonal.

They skipped the door just past the top of the stairs, and Lindsey didn't show her inside.

"What's that room?" Cara asked.

"Just a broom closet." Lindsey led Cara past a quaint bathroom with a claw foot tub but no shower, then by another bedroom, and finally to the last door at the end of the hallway.

"This is my room," Lindsey said timidly. "I hope you like it."

"I'm sure I'll love it." She gave the little girl a squeeze on the shoulder. Lindsey swung open the door, and Cara gasped.

"Is something wrong?" Lindsey asked, insecurity lacing her words.

"Oh no." Cara quickly covered up her surprise. She'd been expecting pinks and purples and Disney princesses like Mattie's and Pari's rooms. Not this. "It's beautiful. Stunning actually. You have exquisite taste." She bit down on her lip. How did you explain taste to a child? "It means—"

"I know what it means." Lindsey frowned. "Go look around."

Once again, Cara stepped back in time to the same era as the parlor downstairs. A canopy bed abutted the wall, burgundy drapes hanging down from the wooden frame. A small side table made of red cherry was next to the bed, accompanied by a large matching wardrobe and dresser with a sheer white scarf draped over the corners of the mirror.

The shades were closed, and the ceiling light was dim, creating shadows around the room. Cara almost went to the window to pull the shades up, but Lindsey jerked her the other way.

"This hope chest is beautiful." Cara knelt down in front of the intricately carved chest pushed up against the bed.

"I have all my treasures in there." Lindsey opened the lid, and Cara made sure not to react to the contents, which were obviously items that had been passed down generation to generation from woman to woman. Only one toy—a doll, lay in the chest, accompanied by a box of ribbons, a tarnished silver brush, and a velvet blue hat with a pink flower.

In fact, Cara saw no other toys in the sterile cool room. "You must keep your room clean. Where are all your toys?"

It was slightly weird, but it fit with the rest of the house.

"In the closet. Daddy makes me put them away."

He must be pretty strict about it.

"This is Gladys. Isn't she pretty?" Lindsey cradled the ancient doll in her arm, twisting a strand of its tangled blonde hair around her finger. The white dress and bonnet had faded to a yellow tint, and the doll had little scratch marks across its cheeks. It had probably been beautiful in its day.

"She is."

Cara glanced up in the darkened mirror over the dresser. It had a crack that hadn't been there earlier. She did a double take at Lindsey's mottled gray face, her eyes blacker than mud, her bobbed hair like moldy straw. Her grin exposed black and yellow teeth, and instead of the sailor dress Lindsey was wearing, the mirror girl wore an old fashioned white dress.

It almost looked like the little girl in the picture downstairs, a dead and decaying version. Cara leaned forward, staring as little prickles of apprehension flickered across her neck. Gladys was in the mirror-Lindsey's hands, except it was a pristine version with silky curly hair and no marks on its cheeks.

Cara blinked, and the appalling image cleared from the mirror. She looked over to Lindsey to find the girl's sparkling blue eyes and pink pudgy cheeks. Cara checked the mirror again, which no longer was cracked, and her and Lindsey's images reflected back.

That had been completely crazy, and she had no idea where that picture had come from. Maybe she was tired or dehydrated. It'd been so hot outside, and Cara had skipped lunch today to get some work done.

"Are you ready to go eat dinner now?" Lindsey smiled, but a flash of the mirror image crossed Cara's mind again, and a small shiver coursed through her.

"Yes, I think I need something to drink. I'm a little dehydrated." *And my imagination is running wild.*

Lindsey took Cara's hand and escorted her downstairs.

Chapter Four

"Oh my gosh, something smells wonderful?" Cara breathed in the delicious smell, letting her guard down even more since they were now downstairs. She had to admit that Lindsey's room was slightly creepy.

"Daddy made a special dish for you. We're celebrating."

"Well, I can't wait to eat." Cara surveyed the meal on the table. Filet mignon, asparagus drowning in hollandaise sauce, and a fresh fruit salad. "How in the world did you have time to make all this?" she asked Kyle.

He shrugged. "You've been up there longer than you realized." He glanced to the window, and Cara followed his gaze.

Wait—it was dark outside. It didn't get dark until seven-thirty. She looked at the clock on the wall to confirm.

Eight o'clock.

It'd been barely past five when she'd gone upstairs with Lindsey. No way had three hours passed. It wasn't possible. She rubbed her forehead. Maybe she'd read the clock wrong.

"Let's eat. Get our drinks, Daddy." Lindsey clapped her hands together, and they were soon seated. Kyle went around the table with a bottle of Merlot. First he filled Cara's glass, then his, then Lindsey's.

Cara pointed to Lindsey's glass. "Don't you think some lemonade would be more appropriate than wine? Maybe some juice?"

"Wine basically is juice." Lindsey smiled sweetly at her, but Kyle kept his eyes on the table. "It's just for making a toast."

Okay, as long as she didn't drink it. But this I'm-an-adult-act was going a bit far, and Cara wasn't impressed with how Kyle let his daughter boss him around. He was probably overcompensating for the loss of her mother, but if he wasn't careful, he'd have an out of control girl by the time she reached her teens.

"A toast." Lindsey picked up the half-full wine glass, which looked like it might topple in her hands any second. Kyle raised his drink, so Cara picked up her own.

Lindsey smiled. "To my new mommy, Cara."

Cara choked on her breath, her face flushing to the shade of the wine. "What?" she finally managed.

"To Cara," Kyle said quietly, and Lindsey's grin grew wider.

What had created this needy little girl? Cara definitely wouldn't be returning. After she finished eating, she would politely explain how love worked and maybe politely suggest to Kyle on her way out that he needed to man up.

"I'm not your mom, Lindsey."

"Not officially." Her bright eyes didn't dim at Cara's scolding tone.

Cara stared as Kyle dished up food for Lindsey. He cut her steak into small pieces and then sliced all her asparagus in half.

"I told you I don't like it that way," Lindsey squealed.

Kyle mumbled an apology and slid the cut asparagus onto his own plate, then dished up more for her.

Um, wow. Okay. Cara often joked that Mattie could get away with murder, but if she had treated her mother like that, Riya would have sent her away from the table. Cara wanted to send Lindsey away at this point.

Lindsey put the glass of wine to her lips.

"What are you doing? No." Cara reached over and grabbed the glass out of Lindsey's small hands, but not before the girl had taken a sip. "Kyle, that's wine."

"I'm old enough." Lindsey pouted, her face darkening and her blue eyes turning to steel. "Daddy, tell Mommy I'm old enough."

"Stop with this, Lindsey. I'm not your mommy."

Kyle drummed his fingers on the table, his tight face cast down.

"What is wrong with you? She can't have wine. She's five." He didn't just need to man up; he needed to bring them both to a therapist. Cara set the glass down, out of reach of Lindsey. "You're the dad, and she's the child, and you need to act like it."

Lindsey's eyes, now almost black, widened, and her mouth twitched—her lips red as blood on her pale face.

The whole house seemed to drop twenty degrees, and something set Cara on edge. It wasn't the icy stare Lindsey was giving her or the nervous energy from her father; there was something intangible, a force or something…

The grisly image of the little girl from the mirror earlier flashed across Lindsey's face: the gray skin, the black eyes, and the yellow teeth. It seemed to flicker in and out.

Cara jumped to her feet. "I'm out of here."

She ran for the door, but before she got outside, she heard Lindsey's voice. "You'll be back."

Cara spun around to see Lindsey staring with quiet curiosity, her father twirling the wine glass in his fingers and watching it like it was the most interesting thing in the world.

She crossed the back porch into the humid night air, and she almost stumbled rushing down the steps. Something was really wrong in that house, and she couldn't blame it on her own dehydration. She wasn't claustrophobic, and she was outside under the night sky, but she'd never felt so trapped as she did now.

(UN)LUCKY THIRTEEN

The short jaunt across the grass looked a hundred miles, but she was almost to the gate when *whack*!

Cara's body hit a flat surface, and she bounced backwards onto the scratchy grass, arms and legs splayed out. She lifted her head and rubbed the tender spot one her forehead as the pain echoed through her.

What happened? It was like she'd hit a wall except there was no wall. The picket fence was only three feet high and couldn't possibly have hit her forehead.

She glanced back at the door, her heart pounding. Kyle and Lindsey watched her from the porch, Lindsey's arms crossed like she was about to reprimand Cara for her silly actions.

Cara scrambled to her feet and reached for the gate, but her hand slammed into a wall.

A wall that shouldn't be there. She tried again to get to the gate, but every time her hand smacked something solid.

"What did you do to me?" Cara screamed, her throat on fire. Maybe they'd drugged her, put something in the lemonade earlier—she hadn't drank any of the wine.

With her fist, she thumped the invisible wall, running along the fence and looking for an opening.

Nothing.

She turned the corner at the back of the lot and squeezed between the fence and the trees, dragging her hand along the wall.

All the way around the lot, around through the deepest part of the backyard and back to the house. She was still barricaded in, even in the front yard just off the sidewalk.

The dark night enveloped her, no stars in sight, the only illumination from the streetlights and the surrounding homes. She fell to her knees.

A couple was walking their dog down a ways, slowly coming in her direction, and she stood, placing her hands on her prison wall.

"Help," she called.

They didn't look her way, absorbed in their conversation.

"Help me, please!" she yelled. They were getting closer, almost to her. Why couldn't they hear her? Why couldn't they see her? Cara slammed her palm against the wall, the thundering noise echoing around her, but they didn't react at all.

They were so close, right there. She could touch them if not for this wall. "Help!" she screamed.

They stopped.

And turned.

Cara almost jumped for joy. She hammered on the wall again, except they only looked down, and Cara's gaze fell to the ground. The dog was pooping, his eyes on Cara as if he saw her. She moved to the right, and his gaze did too.

(UN)LUCKY THIRTEEN

The man bent down, scooped up the poop with a plastic baggie, and tugged at the dog. It whined, still staring at Cara.

"Help me!" she tried again, but the man led the dog away, and she was alone.

Tears streamed down her cheeks. The people were gone, and she was trapped with this crazy kid and her do-nothing father. She didn't know what was going on or why, but she just wanted out.

Cara fell to her knees and tumbled forward, slamming into the invisible wall.

Everything went black.

Chapter Five

A warm washcloth rested on Cara's throbbing head, and a gentle hand traced lines up and down her arm. What a horrible dream that had been.

"There, there," a voice said softly. "Everything will be okay, Mommy."

Cara stiffened, the voice becoming recognizable.

"You need to rest. You got a little bump on your head," Lindsey said.

Cara touched her forehead to find a small lump at her hairline. The rag was pulled away, and the bright light blinded Cara, making her squint. Her surroundings came into focus.

She was sitting on the chaise lounge in the parlor, Lindsey hovering on the edge. "I don't know why you tried to leave me. I told you you're my new mommy."

"Let me go. Why are you doing this?" Cara's voice shook with fear. She didn't know who Lindsey and Kyle were or what they wanted, but maybe she could reason with them.

"I wanted another mommy. It's been too long since my last one. And Daddy is so lonely."

An icy fist gripped Cara's heart. She didn't want to ask, but she had to. "What happened to your mom?"

"Which one? There's been so many." Lindsey looked to the window brimming with sunshine and sighed.

Cara zeroed in on the picture in the middle of the wall of portraits. Earlier the girl in the photograph had seemed similar to Lindsey, but now they appeared to be an exact match. The picture girl's hair was different, no longer the original bob it had been, and she was wearing Lindsey's sailor dress. Cara blinked, and the image went back to normal.

"Or do you mean my first," Lindsey said. The warm hand rested on Cara's arm once again, but her voice tightened into a snarl. "Papa killed her. Spiked her lemonade with arsenic. He meant for me to die too, but I was too smart for him. I found out his plan and switched my lemonade with Molly's."

"He… he… tried to murder you? Kyle?" *Oh god, he's going to kill me too.* She whipped her head around. He stood at the mantle rearranging the fake pinecones.

"Not him. My real father," Lindsey huffed and crossed her arms. "Molly was a perfect angel," she spat. "Molly was smart and beautiful."

Cara had to get out of this crazy home and away from this wacko family. Maybe if she pretended everything was okay, she could attempt an escape again. Maybe that invisible wall wasn't there anymore.

"Was Molly your mom?" she asked.

"No." Lindsey scowled. "She was my older sister, the perfect child, and Papa chose for her to live and me to die. He took his own life when he realized what he'd done though. He poisoned his little angel." Lindsey smiled gleefully.

Nothing about this seemed real. Cara glanced up at the pictures on the wall, at the one in the middle of the little girl from over a hundred years ago. An exact copy of the girl in front of her except with different hair. It couldn't be Lindsey in that picture.

"When were you born?" Cara choked out.

"1906. Do you like my picture? Mama had it taken the year before Papa tried to murder us."

No, it wasn't possible. She wasn't in the room with a five-year-old who was over a hundred years old.

"These are all my other mommies." Lindsey swept her hand out to showcase the pictures. "I've had a lot of mommies since 1906. Some of them were nicer than others."

Cara's mouth ran dry. How many women had been in this home? This couldn't be real. But Lindsey's vocabulary and the way she acted, her room, and that creepy girl in the mirror…Cara swallowed the rock in her throat.

(UN)LUCKY THIRTEEN

"Where did they go?" Cara clenched her hands to keep them from trembling.

"To the basement. You won't go there though if you're a good mommy."

Cara stared through the doorway that led down that small hallway. A low sound started in her ears and grew to a steady drumbeat.

Thump, thump, thump.

She covered her ears, but the sound only seemed to get louder until it pulsed through her whole body. Her cheeks burned, and her throat tightened. They would kill her, and she'd never see her family again.

Even though Lindsey said Kyle wasn't her real father, he would obviously do anything Lindsey wanted. He'd bury her in the back, and nobody would know. Nobody would realize she was gone for a few days, and she'd be dead and rotting in the garden.

Cara shot to her feet and took off for the door. She had to try to escape again. There had to be a break in the wall, and she had missed it.

Lindsey appeared right in front of her. Cara turned for the steps to the grand staircase. She could crawl out a window onto the porch roof and drop to the ground or shout for someone to help. Those people had probably been too involved in their conversation to notice her. The dog had.

Cara sprinted for the stairs.

"Come back!" Lindsey called.

No way, no how. A burst of energy propelled Cara up the steps.

She hit the second floor and paused for a second. Lindsey's shrill yell wafted up the staircase again, accompanied by footsteps, and Cara took off down the hall to get to the front facing rooms that were over the porch.

She fisted her clammy hands and pumped her arms as she turned around the first corner and then the second. She skidded to a stop on the wood floors and stared down the long hallway. She should be at the front of the house, but there was no door. Just a long looming, shadowy hallway.

What the ever living heck. All the doors had disappeared.

"Cara," Lindsey's voice echoed softly in her ears.

Cara dashed down the hall, running as fast as she could. She turned the corner and found another long hallway, but she didn't stop. Her feet thundered on the wood floor as she ran, searching for a way out. On and on. She had to have circled the upstairs several times by now.

The low and threatening beat she felt downstairs started up again, the pressure invading her body. She had to get out of the house. There had to be some kind of escape.

But each doorless hallway led to another, and the thumping pounded in her head and heart. In all this time she'd been running, she hadn't passed the stairs once. Where had they gone?

Her aching muscles begged her to stop, but she kept going, taking deep breaths. She would not allow Lindsey to trap her here.

But what if she couldn't get out? What did Lindsey want from her? Why would she want to kill Cara? They'd just met.

"Cara!" The scream rang through the hallway, and Cara dropped to her knees gasping for breath. There was no escape. "I need you to come back," Lindsey's voice softened, sounding more like the little girl she might have been.

"What do you want from me?" Cara called back. She couldn't keep running on this endless loop.

"I need you to be my mommy. I need a mommy," the voice begged.

There was nowhere to go. She had no choice.

"Okay. I'll come back. I'm going to the bathroom first." Cara had to find her wits so she could figure out what to do next. She had to take a few moments and get a drink to cool her body down.

Cara crawled to her feet, and a wave of vertigo passed through her. The doors of the empty hallway had suddenly appeared, and she blinked to focus. The bathroom was down from her, and she quickly slipped inside.

She stared at the mirror at her red face and then splashed some water on her hot skin. It did little to cool her down, and she examined the rest of the room.

The block glass windows would be impossible to break out. She'd need something big and heavy to crash them.

She had to leave the bathroom and go back to Lindsey. If Cara pretended to comply with Lindsey's wishes, she could find her way out.

She crept into the hall and to the next door. Lindsey was nowhere in sight, and Cara grabbed the knob and turned it softly. Just as she got it open, she remembered this was a broom closet.

But no. Light peeked through the crack in the doorway, so Lindsey pushed the door open farther and stepped inside to find a bedroom similar to Lindsey's. Faded wallpaper covered the walls, and a dresser held a brush and small mirror, a small blue ball, and an unfinished cross-stitch project. The air was stuffy.

Cara shut the door behind her.

Three dolls lay at the top of the bed on a plush pillow and a white blanket with violet and yellow flowers.

"Mommy." Lindsey pounded on the door. "Come back, I need you."

The dolls were beautiful. The middle one looked more like a baby, with its shiny molded head and hair covered by a bonnet. Its satiny white gown was edged with lace. The two dolls flanking the baby were older looking. The right had brown ringlets hanging to its shoulders, bright blue eyes, and a pretty peach dress with a white apron. The one on the left had soft blonde hair with a maroon velvety hat matching her dress and boots.

Cara reached out to touch one of the dolls, but a noise clattered at the window. She spun around.

Rain.

"Mommy, mommy?" Lindsey thrashed at the door, kicking it now.

Cara needed to find her way out of this house. She ran toward the window but froze a few feet away.

The rain crashing down was red, deep red. And thick. The drops hit the pane and slowly slid down, like they were heavy, and the air filled with the metallic tang of blood.

Lindsey's screams intensified, but she was no longer pounding on the door. Cara reached out her hand. The red rain battered the window, the roof, the side of the house, and the room heated like an oven.

She backed up, unable to take her eyes off the window, until she slammed into the wall.

"Mommy," Lindsey said quietly from the other side.

"I… I…" Cara grabbed the doorknob and twisted it, but something caught her eye. A figure with a somber face sitting on the corner of the bed, a child in a long-sleeved lavender dress with a pink ribbon around the waist.

Lindsey's face framed by long black hair.

No, the nose was straighter, the mouth wider. This girl was older, a teenager, and had hair in braids and a less cutesy dress.

The girl just sat there, and Cara tugged on her tightening collar, her heart racing as the blood rain pummeled the house. A crack of thunder boomed, and lightning lit up the room. The girl disappeared, the bed empty except for the three dolls. Cara didn't want to move, didn't want to think. Her breaths came out quick and ragged.

Eyes were on her, drilling into her from somewhere, but she couldn't see anyone... Only felt them.

The lights flickered, the room still a sauna, and a laugh echoed from the empty corner. The hackles rose on Cara's neck. The laugh then came from the closet. Then from under the bed. Cara's head whipped around, the terror rising inside her. It was everywhere!

She swung the door open and stumbled into the hallway, gasping for breath. The air was clear and the temperature cool. Cara tugged the door shut and slumped against the wall.

This room... She drew her gaze up. This room was the only one Lindsey hadn't shown her.

Cara stared down the empty hallway, waiting for her head and heart to slow down. The doors had once again disappeared. What was going on?

A hand touched her shoulder, and she jumped.

Kyle stood next to her, his head hanging and his hands in his pockets. "Sorry."

"What's going on?" Cara choked out. Ghosts weren't real, but that's what Lindsey had to be. But she had felt real and solid any time Cara had touched her. Was Kyle a ghost too? "Who are you?"

"I'm like you. I made a delivery to the house, and I got trapped too." He knelt down next to her, and she put a few more inches of space between them.

"But why? What does she want with us?" Cara gazed down the hallway, but there still were no doors.

"We need to have a baby. Then she'll let us go." He said it so seriously like he'd already accepted it as truth.

"A baby? Me and you?" No way would she have sex with Kyle. She didn't even know the guy. "And what would a baby do?"

Here she'd thought he wasn't a great dad and all, and now Lindsey wanted them to have a baby together. But that couldn't be true.

This whole thing was messed up. No normal guy would tell a story like that to get a woman to have sex with him.

"It will give Lindsey a new chance at life. She can take over the child's body." His haunted brown eyes begged her to believe him.

Cara stared at her feet. "Why wasn't she able to get out yet? It's over a hundred years since she died. Well, I assumed she died."

Kyle shrugged. "I think a lot of years passed before she tried. Her body is small, but her mind has grown and learned over the years. She tried adopting other moms, but that didn't work."

"The basement?" Cara's throat went dry, and Kyle nodded. Lindsey probably piled up the bodies of the people who couldn't help her, probably killed them when they became useless, and she would add Cara to the pile soon.

"The best thing to do is to produce that baby for her. Then we'll be free."

Produce. She almost scoffed. As if it were that easy anyway. Riya was only a few years older than Cara, but she'd had problems getting pregnant and had needed help to have Pari. Not everybody got pregnant off their first try.

There would be no first try though.

"I'm not having sex with you." Cara glared at him, and a few puzzle pieces clicked together in her head. He had to be lying; he'd say anything to get out of the house. "You'll be free, but I won't. I'll be pregnant for nine months and then what? Huh?" She poked him in the shoulder, her voice hard.

And Lindsey wouldn't want to take over the body of a helpless infant, making herself dependent and weak. No, she'd wait until that baby was older.

(UN)LUCKY THIRTEEN

For frick's sake. She couldn't really be talking about Lindsey taking over the body of a baby. None of that was real. But if it was… What would happen? Would that child die when Lindsey took its body?

Cara's child.

She pushed by Kyle and took off down the hall, rounded the corner, and found the stairway. Each step down, her foot felt heavier and heavier.

Lindsey stood at the bottom and flung her arms out around Cara's waist. "I missed you, Mommy. Don't do that again."

Cara looked over Lindsey's head and out the front window. Dusk had settled without a cloud in the sky. The blood rain from upstairs wasn't real either, but she didn't know how it had happened.

"I missed you too." Cara patted Lindsey on the head. Best to keep the girl thinking they were on the same side.

Lindsey led Cara over to the couch, and they sat next to each other. "Did Daddy explain it all? I can't wait for you to have a baby."

"But that baby will die when you take over its body. How can you do that to another child?"

"How could my father try to kill me? Is that fair? Is it fair I didn't get to live a full life and have been stuck in this small body in this house?" Lindsey wacked the couch with a throw pillow. "I've been here by myself for a long time, and all I want is a chance for life." She slumped down in

46

her seat, her face dark. "I thought finding a mommy would let me grow, but it never worked. They never wanted to stick around either, but now there're here forever." Her lips twitched into a smile, and she stared through the doorway to the hall.

"Why me?" Cara asked.

Lindsey clutched her arm and snuggled into her side. "You were so friendly. And you're pretty. And I knew Daddy would like you."

"Why do you keep calling him Daddy? He's not your father."

"Because families are made up of mommies and daddies and their children. And we will have such a fun life together. I need to wait until the baby is older before I take over her body."

"What if it's a boy?"

Lindsey laughed and patted Cara's thigh. "It won't be. Don't worry."

If it were a boy, Lindsey would make them do it again and again till she got that girl.

Cara had to try to escape again. Maybe tonight after everyone went to sleep. She faked a yawn and covered her mouth. "I'm really tired. I think I need to go to bed."

It wasn't a lie; she was exhausted.

"Great." Lindsey slid off the couch. "I'll show you to yours and Daddy's room."

(UN)LUCKY THIRTEEN

"What?" No way was she sharing a room with Kyle. "I… I need my own room. I mean it's my first night here and all." And she didn't want to sleep in bed with a man she hardly knew. Kyle might be desperate to escape, and he might try something.

Lindsey stomped her foot. "Mommy!"

"Please. I'm so tired." This time a real yawn stretched Cara's face.

"Okay," she relented.

Lindsey accompanied Cara upstairs to the bathroom and gave her some clothes. Cara didn't ask how she'd gotten clothes that were the correct size. She had no desire to find out more right now. *Cara's* bedroom was on the opposite side of the house from Lindsey's room, and that was just fine with her.

She climbed into bed and under the heavy quilt. She would play Lindsey's game while she figured out how to escape.

Because she would escape. There was no doubt about that.

Chapter Six

"I love this book." Lindsey cuddled up to Cara the next day on the swing on the back porch. It would be so easy to wrap her hands around Lindsey's delicate neck, but Cara could never do that, never kill a child. Who knew if Lindsey could even be killed.

Lindsey had prepared a delicious breakfast for her, so obviously Kyle wasn't the only one who cooked around here. It was amazing how Lindsey bounced back and forth between a little girl and the maturity of an old woman.

Cara opened the *Anne of Green Gables* book and started the next chapter.

She had crept out of the house early in the morning, but when she went outside, she hit that same invisible wall she had earlier. She'd even tried hitting it with a large rock, but she couldn't break through. There had to be some way out though.

They finished the chapter, and Cara shut the book. She needed to learn about Lindsey and her history. Maybe that would give her some insight into what to do.

"Read more," Lindsey pouted, but Cara said no.

"I want to learn more about you." She patted Lindsey's head. "Tell me more about your family."

Lindsey leaned back into the cushions and sighed. "Mama was wonderful. We baked bread together, and I helped her in the garden. They planted all the trees back here. The yard was empty when I was small."

The tree-filled yard had seemed so inviting and private when Cara first saw it, but now it felt stifling.

"I bet you played outside a lot."

"I did. Papa chastised me because I brought dirt into the house, but Mama didn't care." Lindsey's body tensed up. "He never got angry with Molly. He never hit her like he hit me and Mama."

Cara pushed against the porch with her foot so the swing rocked. "He hit you?" She mustered up some sympathy for the little girl Lindsey used to be, but she was no longer that girl. She was the kidnapper who imprisoned Cara in this horrible house.

"Only when he was angry." She held still for a few moments. "Well, he hit Molly sometimes, but not as much as me."

"Is that why you killed your sister?" Cara held her breath, not knowing if Lindsey would answer. She'd said she'd switched the poisoned drinks so that Molly would take it. She should have just dumped it out.

"I didn't kill her. Papa did. He prepared the drinks with the arsenic, and I handed mine off to Molly because I saw what he had done. They'd warned me enough times that the arsenic could kill us, and then he gave it to me to drink. He wanted me gone, so I made sure he lost what he wanted the most." Lindsey giggled. "She got so sick, and Papa realized what he'd done." Her maniacal laughs came harder. "She deserved it. I hate her so much."

What the eff was wrong with this girl? Did Kyle know all this? He'd disappeared after breakfast, probably glad Cara could take Lindsey off his hands.

Cara didn't know what to say, so she remained quiet until Lindsey popped her head up. "Mama was wonderful. Do you remember that doll in my chest? She gave that to me on my fifth birthday. She gave it to me even though Papa said I didn't deserve it. Even though he gave Molly three dolls, and she wouldn't share. She got mad when I touched the beautiful brown curls of her favorite doll, and then I got in trouble."

Cara thought back to the dolls, and the one with the brown ringlets in the peach dress. Molly's dolls. She sucked in a hard breath. There was a teenager in braids in that room she'd been in.

"How old was Molly when she died?"

"Thirteen. She was so mean to me." Lindsey rambled on about her sister, but Cara paid no attention. The girl in the lavender dress might have been thirteen, and she looked like Lindsey, but ghosts weren't real.

But then again, neither were invisible walls that kept you trapped or girls over a hundred years old.

"Does Molly have long black hair?"

Lindsey's head whipped around. "You saw her?" Her voice trembled slightly, and her eyes darted around. "She's a liar. Don't listen to her. She lies all the time."

"I didn't talk to her. I only saw her for a moment." The fear in Lindsey's voice put Cara on edge. This ghost/demon, whatever-Lindsey was, was scared of something. Of her sister maybe. God, if Molly's ghost scared Lindsey, then Molly had to be ten times worse.

"Don't go in there again." Lindsey stared up at Cara with wide eyes. "She'll try hurt you like she tried to hurt me."

"I won't." Cara didn't need two ghost girls threatening her. The thought would almost be funny if it wasn't so real. "Did Molly know your father was going to kill you?"

Lindsey stared off over the yard. "Yes, she wanted me gone too."

"But how did you die?" Cara asked. Lindsey was five, so she must have died soon after.

"The lemonade wasn't the only thing he poisoned. I ate some pudding sitting on the counter after Papa killed himself, and then I got sick too." Lindsey said nothing for a moment and then seized Cara's hand. "Let's go out to the garden."

They walked down the steps hand-in-hand into the lush grass. A bee buzzed by Cara's side, and a car horn honked down the street. This backyard seemed so normal, but it wasn't, and Cara would not give up yet. There had to be a way out.

Maybe she needed to talk to Kyle. He might give her more clues.

Chapter Seven

"I'm going to go in the backyard to my swing." Lindsey grinned at Kyle and Cara as she lit the candles at the table set with wine in the crystal goblets and a fancy meal served on fine china. "You two can enjoy your time together, and maybe we'll have a new little baby around here in nine months." She winked and scuttled to the drawer to put the lighter away.

Cara stared at her retreating figure, not understanding this girl. She was a hundred years old and seemed so wise in some ways but in others was so naïve. Cara was not going to have sex with Kyle, and Lindsey couldn't make her.

She gripped the stem of the wine glass. Could she?

The girl had imprisoned her in this house and supposedly all those other women. Maybe Lindsey had killed them when they didn't produce babies. She swallowed the bitter wine and finally looked up to Kyle, who was stuffing his mouth. This was their first time really alone together since she arrived. Lindsey had been around every second, only giving Cara a few minutes' relief when she ran to the bathroom.

"How long have you been here?" she asked.

"It's hard to tell because the days sometimes seem to run together, but about a month I think." Kyle's face scrunched up. "It was the day after Independence Day when I stopped by."

The Fourth of July? That couldn't be.

"It's the last week of September," she said, and he about dropped his fork.

"I've been here for three months?" He swallowed hard. "It's messed up. She needs two people to give her a baby, and I've waited forever for someone to come in. It's just a baby, and we can leave."

Did he not hear a word Cara said earlier? Lindsey might allow him to leave, but she wouldn't let Cara go.

"What happens if we don't?"

Kyle's eyes widened, and his gaze darted to the window overlooking the back. "You don't want to defy her." He closed his eyes and twisted his napkin into a tight roll. "I don't want to die."

"She can't really kill us. She's five." The words were a lie though. Cara wasn't sure what she was capable of.

He stared at her, and her face heated, and then Kyle jumped to his feet and dragged Cara out of her chair. He tugged her into the hall with the door to the basement and flung it open.

"This is what happened when I told you no that second time you stopped. Lindsey was already upset that you couldn't come in that first time. And then when I sent you away…" He peered down into the darkness.

An oppressive heat enveloped Cara, the steps disappearing into a black hole of nothingness. A slow beat started in her heart and grew until she felt the thumping in her ears. Whatever was down there wasn't good. It was horrible. Evil.

"Don't go," a quiet voice said in her head. Cara looked for Lindsey, but she wasn't around.

Kyle reached to turn on the light, and she slapped at his hand. "We don't need to go down there."

"No, you're going." He flipped the light on. Nothing but the rickety steps were visible, and Kyle started down.

Cara held her breath and took a tentative step. Then another and another. She gripped the railing and kept her gaze cast down, not wanting to look even though she knew he'd make her. But it wasn't just him. It was like an invisible force was tugging on her heart, encouraging her to descend into the furnace of a basement.

Kyle stepped away from the landing, and she went down the last stair.

"Look," he begged.

The musty decaying smell slammed into her, almost making her gag, and Cara tilted her head up. When she saw the sight in front of her, she about jumped back into the wall. The basement was empty except for the few pieces of furniture. Two long couches, a love seat, and several different types of chairs. Each of them held one or more bodies. She did a quick count: twelve.

Their clothes were all intact right down to the shoes and jewelry. One of the skeletons even had a bright red hat on her head. All of them were in different states of decay, and the rotting smell of flesh seemed to grow stronger and stronger the more she stood there. Some skeletons were only bones covered by clothing, but other bodies still had their skin—shrunken and gray, and their straw-like hair. Just like the pictures upstairs, the clothes came from a variety of decades.

"How did they die?" she choked out.

A scream ripped through the air, and Cara reached for Kyle, looking around for the source, but she couldn't see where it was coming from. Another sounded and then a third. And then the screams started to overlap, getting louder and louder. Screams of endless pain and torture and sorrow.

"What's going on?" Cara yelled, but Kyle didn't answer. The hair on the back of her neck stood, and she felt something on her arm. Cara yelped and brushed it off, but there was nothing there. Something touched her other arm, like little fingers grasping for her. The screams intensified along with the pressure on her feet, then her ankles.

(UN)LUCKY THIRTEEN

Cara shot up the steps, the noise following her. She couldn't feel the little fingers on her skin anymore, but she swore someone was grabbing for her. Maybe Kyle. She ran through the door and skidded to a stop behind Kyle. He'd gone up before her.

"I… What was that? I thought you were behind me." Cara gasped for breath, relieved that the screams had gone away.

He shook his head frantically and slammed the door shut. Cara collapsed on the floor and watched the basement door. What if they escape? What if they tried to kill her?

"That's where you and I will end up if we don't make a baby." Kyle wrung his hands, his face pale.

Those women. Lindsey had killed them and trapped them in their own private hell. So many souls were stuck in this house, and Cara would be one of them if she wasn't careful

Chapter Eight

"Did you have fun together?" Lindsey asked, a twinkle in her eye. She sat in the parlor with Cara an hour after the horrible trip to the basement. Kyle was watching TV, and Cara heard him laugh. She wasn't sure how he could laugh at anything right now, especially after being in that basement. Cara still felt grimy and gross, could still feel the little fingers on her skin.

"Yes, I did. Kyle is a terrific man." She would string Lindsey along as long as possible.

"Did he kiss you?" Lindsey squirmed in her seat, her excitement palpable.

The images of the dead bodies and the screams of horror and pain ran through Cara's head, and she gritted her teeth. The smell of rotting flesh seemed to charge the air.

Not in your life.

"Those types of things take time, but we're on the right track." She patted Lindsey's arm.

(UN)LUCKY THIRTEEN

"I don't want it to take too long," Lindsey pouted. "I'm ready to grow up. Besides, it'll be a few more years until I can have the body for myself."

"I know you are. But you need to let this happen naturally between me and your daddy."

"You know what happens if you don't make me a baby." Lindsey's voice took on a hard edge, and she turned her head in the direction of the basement door.

Cara swallowed at the growing lump in her throat. Did Lindsey know they'd been down there? Did all those dead women talk to her?

Cara could be one of them. Lindsey would place her body among the others, and she would slowly deteriorate, flesh rotting away to the bone. And when Lindsey led another victim to the basement of horrors, Cara's ghost would scream as the others had, for release from the hell she'd been placed in.

"I've always wanted children. A baby might be the thing to bring some life back into this house." Cara cringed inwardly at her words, but Lindsey sighed contentedly.

"I want to show you something up in my room." Lindsey crawled off the couch, took Cara's hand, and led her upstairs.

The door to Cara's room was the only one that lay open, and Lindsey motioned to it and stopped. "Maybe it's time you move into Daddy's room."

It had been one night. One flipping night.

"Not yet, but soon."

She'd keep brushing Lindsey off as long as she could.

"Why aren't you in the big room?" Cara asked. Kyle was in one of the other bedrooms, but the master was empty.

"Because that was Mama's room. She wouldn't be happy if I took it over. Besides," Lindsey said, gripping Cara's hand as they passed another closed door, Molly's door. "I like my room best."

Lindsey knelt down in front of the hope chest and dug out some sort of scrapbook. She flipped it open and sat down, back against the chest. "This is a ticket from the circus. It was amazing. They had dancing horses, and a man walked across a beam, and oh, the elephants. Have you been to a circus?"

"Yes, many years ago." And it was probably much different from the one Lindsey attended.

She turned the page to some very fragile pressed flowers. "Mama gave this to me on my fourth birthday. It's a special flower she grew only for me."

Cara resisted the urge to crumble the dried petals into dust. "What type of flower is it?"

"I don't know. Mama probably told me, but I forgot. I was only four."

A cloud covered the sun outside, and the light in the room dimmed.

(UN)LUCKY THIRTEEN

"How does all this work? How have you lived here all these years and nobody knows about you?" Somebody had to have noticed the little girl who never grew up.

Lindsey's face darkened, and her head fell. "Because of what Papa did, they tore down the house. Nobody cared that we were still here. Not the neighbors. Not my mama's friends."

"We? Are your parents here too?"

"No," she scowled. "Me and Molly. But you must never go see her. She will take you away from me. She will hurt you." Lindsey's eyes drilled into Cara, and she nodded.

Lindsey flipped forward a few pages and pointed to a drawing done in pencil. "This is our house. Isn't it beautiful? It's so much nicer than the one here now."

Cara stared at the picture, the same house that had first stolen her attention. "What do you mean?"

Lindsey huffed. "They built a different house, and another family moved in. So many families have come and gone through the years. I can pass into their house. It's how I've learned, watching that infernal TV when they have it on. Well, until we got ours. Daddy was so much more agreeable after I got it."

Nothing Lindsey was saying made any sense. She'd just said somebody tore down their house.

"You're saying that at this exact moment, there's another family in another house on this same lot?"

"Yes, we both exist in the same space. Very few people will see my home though, and those that do are special. Like you." Lindsey patted Cara's arm tenderly. "You were meant to be my mommy."

Cara tried to process it all, that she was living in a house that was no longer there. And somehow, in another dimension, or whatever, a family was here too. Eating dinner, sleeping, and living their lives knowing nothing about Cara or Kyle or Lindsey.

But wait. All this time she'd been here, and she'd only used the bathroom once. That was impossible. She couldn't go that long without peeing. And she wasn't sure now that she'd seen Kyle or Lindsey use a bathroom at all either.

Oh no. Lindsey had already killed her, and she was trapped here like the poor souls in the basement. It wasn't another dimension; it was a place between heaven and hell.

"Am I dead already?" she choked out.

"No," Lindsey laughed. "How could you have a baby if you're dead?"

"But I haven't used the bathroom. And I haven't felt hungry once even though I've eaten."

"You're not dead. The rules here are different." Lindsey patted Cara's arm again. "Don't worry so much, Mommy. I'm taking care of you."

Lindsey flipped to a new page, one that held a black and white picture of a family standing in front of the house—this house. Mother and father stood behind two girls in frilly dresses, the man in a suit. The mother wore a stern look, but the youngest girl, Lindsey, smiled brightly.

Cara couldn't see the expressions of the father or oldest sister because of their blackened faces, but the older sister had long dark hair that hung to her shoulders like the girl in the bedroom.

"Isn't she beautiful?" Lindsey gazed at the photograph and ran her finger alongside her mother's face. "She spent hours working on my hair, getting the curls just right. Papa complained because he thought Mama ignored Molly to help me, but Molly didn't want to look beautiful like I did. She didn't want to take the picture at all."

Lindsey scowled down at the page. "She was always complaining about me. She claimed she didn't know Papa would kill Mama and me, but she's a liar. She said she didn't even want to go with Papa because she didn't like his attention. She was full of nothing but lies. Papa took her into his room for their special time, but she never let me go too. *You don't want to be his special girl,* she'd say. And whenever Papa offered to give me my baths, Molly got in between us, and he forgot about me."

Cara stared at the little girl, stunned. Their special time in his room, his special girl… She gulped at the thought. Maybe that meant a different thing back in Lindsey's day.

Probably not.

"Maybe she was trying to help you."

"Help?" Lindsey spit, the venom strong in her voice. She slammed the book shut. "She got to sleep in his bed and wear Mama's fancy nightgown when Mama was away visiting my grandparents. I was scared one night when it was storming, and Mama was gone. All I wanted was Papa to comfort me, but she threw me out of their room and shut the door on me." Lindsey sniffed.

Cara's stomach soured. Their father was a monster who deserved his horrific death, and she hoped he suffered as he died.

"Are you taking her side?" Lindsey hurled the book into the cedar chest and flung the lid down. Her gaze zeroed in on Cara, and the hairs pricked up on Cara's skin. The room darkened, the sky suddenly black. A burst of lightening flashed through the sky, and the air became hot and heavy.

Lindsey's blonde hair turned into black straw, her face pale with yellow eyes. Cara scrambled back and slammed into the wall.

"Don't you dare take her side." Lindsey shot to her feet and stomped over. Cara quivered under her intense anger. She was going to die. Right here, right now. From a five-year-old demon ghost.

"Please. I'm not. She's a liar, like you said," Cara blurted. "I… I think she trapped me in her room the other day. I thought it was my imagination, so I didn't tell you, but I think she spoke to me. She said not to believe you."

(UN)LUCKY THIRTEEN

The lies spilled out. Cara had to convince Lindsey she was on her side and that she'd stay away from Molly. "I'm sorry."

"I told you she doesn't tell the truth," Lindsey's voice softened, and her hair and eyes turned to normal, the color returning to her cheeks. "You can't trust her."

Sunlight streamed in through the window once again, and the black clouds disappeared.

"I think you should go to your room and think about this," Lindsey said. "Mommies need to trust their daughters."

Cara hung her head. "I will."

She needed that quiet time to think. She slowly crawled to her feet and backed out of the room, not wanting to turn her back on Lindsey. Cara shut the door and started down the hall.

"Cara," Lindsey called, but when Cara turned around, Lindsey's door was shut.

"Come inside," the quiet voice whispered.

Cara stood in front of Molly's door, picturing the room and the girl in the lavender dress clearly, and she reached for the doorknob. Molly hadn't been scary at all, not like Lindsey sometimes was.

"What are you doing?" Kyle gasped. "You're not going in there. You can't."

Why?

But she knew why. Molly would hurt her.

"I wasn't. I don't know what I was doing. I didn't mean to go in." She hadn't, and she couldn't explain why she'd grabbed for the door.

Kyle tugged on her arm and led her down the hall. "Did she tell you how Molly killed a couple of the women? They'd wandered into her room, and she murdered them. She's vicious."

"And Lindsey isn't?"

"But Molly is worse." He started down the steps, and she followed.

"Have you ever seen her?"

"Nope. I'm not going in there." He spun on the step, and she nearly stumbled into him. "And you shouldn't either." Kyle placed his hand on her cheek. "I like you, Cara, and I think this could work between us."

He leaned in and kissed her, his lips warm and soft. She broke it off.

No way was it going to go any further. Cara needed time to figure this out, to maybe escape the house before Lindsey forced them together. There had to be a way out because Lindsey said she'd watched TV in the real house that sat on this property. If Lindsey passed over to that house, then Cara could too.

She put her hands on his shoulders. "Lindsey told me to have some quiet time in my room, so that's where I'm going." She turned around, not bothering to listen for his response.

Chapter Nine

Cara took another bite of the sandwich. One week had passed since Lindsey trapped her here, and even though she technically didn't need to eat, the food Kyle made was scrumptious.

Cooking seemed to be his thing, his time-waster, because there was so little to do around the house. He even dressed up the sandwich and fries with a pickle spear. She chewed another delectable bite and stared at the sandwich.

"Where does the food come from?" she asked.

He shrugged. "It's not real. Just like most things in this house. I go to the fridge to get the meat, and it's there, along with my favorite beer. If you went to the pantry, you'd probably find the things you like too."

"That's so weird." She thought about the other house that was occupying this space in the real world. "Have you ever seen the other family that lives here? Were they the ones you were supposed to deliver the package to?"

He slumped in his chair and slid his plate away. "The box was big, so I set it down and rang the bell. The door opened, a woman, but she didn't see me. Everything kind of flickered, and then there was this little girl in front of me. She was crying, and I stepped into the house thinking she was hurt. Then boom—I'm trapped. I haven't seen the other woman since though."

Lindsey bounded up to the table. "I moved your things into Daddy's room." She smiled, all proud of herself, and something clicked in Cara's head. The closet in her bedroom. There were always clothes in her style that fit her. Shoes too for when she ventured outside. It was like the food that just appeared.

She shook off the thought and focused on Lindsey. "I'm not—"

Kyle laid a hand on her arm. "That's great. Thank you. Why don't you go play in the backyard, and as soon as we're done with dishes, we'll come out."

"Okay." Lindsey took off for the door, slamming it behind her as children do.

Cara crossed her arms and scowled at him. "We're not having sex."

As much as she feared the basement, she wasn't at the point of giving up yet. She would stand her ground.

"You don't have to. And, Cara. I would never make you. But you saw the basement and experienced a little of her power, and there are worse things she can do." His face paled, and his gaze dropped. He remained still, seemingly lost in some horrible memory. "We need to at least pretend.

The bedroom is big. And along with the bed, there's one of those fancy long chairs like in the parlor."

"The chaise lounge."

"Yes," he said, nodding. "And if you're not comfortable sleeping—and only sleeping—in the bed with me, I'll sleep on the um… chaise lounge."

He was a good guy, he'd tried to get her to stay away, and he could have forced her to have sex, but he didn't; he was thrown in a horrible situation like she was, and not once in this last week had she asked him what he'd gone through. He'd brought her to the basement to show her what Lindsey was capable of. He had to be strong to do that because Cara would not willingly go down to that basement again.

"Thank you."

They sat for a few quiet moments until he pushed from the table and stood. "Would you like to go outside with her while I do the dishes?"

She laughed. "No way. I'll help. It's not like I really want to hang out with her anyway."

"Wash or dry?" he asked.

She shrugged. "Dry, I guess." She found a towel and stood next to him as he filled up the sink. "So what did she do to you? I mean, when you first got here?"

"Well, the wall. Once I figured that out, she threw me down into the basement." He grew quiet and stared out the back window. "All those women, the dead bodies, they seemed to come alive. They were reaching for me and begging me for help. I felt their cold rotting flesh against my skin, and they became more agitated and tugged on my shirt or my pant leg. I felt like they were going to tear me apart."

Cara shut off the water, the sink almost full. "How did you get out of there?"

He sighed. "Every time I tried to go up the steps, I'd reach the top and be down at the bottom again with them all clawing at me. Finally I got out, and Lindsey explained how I was her new dad and if I wanted to stay out of the basement, I'd better do as she asked."

He grabbed a plate and started washing. Cara remembered the stench of rotting flesh, the dead bodies, the pain of the women trapped downstairs. She couldn't end up down there too.

"Tell me more about yourself," Cara said. "Do you have a family who's missing you?" The ache inside grew. She might never see her parents or brothers again. It wasn't something she wanted to think about.

"Yeah." Kyle nodded sadly.

They did the dishes, and he told her more about himself, and she shared some things with him too. At least she would have one friend inside this house.

Just as they were finishing, Lindsey poked her head inside. "Mommy, will you run to my room and get my parasol before you come out? It's under my bed."

"Sure." And she would take her time.

Kyle went outside, and Cara headed upstairs. As she was passing Molly's bedroom, she felt a little tug on her heart.

"Come in," a quiet voice said.

Cara spun around. The voice was a girl, light and airy, and it didn't belong to Lindsey. Nobody was in the hallway though. Maybe it had been her imagination.

But no, she knew who it was, and she rushed down the hall.

In Lindsey's room, she kneeled on the floor in front of the bed, the ruffle from the bed skirt hanging down. She pictured herself lifting it and finding the glowing green eyes of Molly. The girl would pounce, her teeth ripping into Cara's neck like a vampire, and the life would slowly drain out of Cara's body.

A cold shiver slithered up her back.

But Lindsey wouldn't send Cara up to her room to be attacked by Molly. Cara held her breath and reached for the bed skirt.

The only thing underneath was dust and a worn parasol. She nabbed it and stood, laughing at herself.

A bang came from across the room as if someone hit the wall, and Cara jumped. She stared at the wall that stood between Lindsey and Molly's room.

"Please," that soft voice said.

Molly was trying to entice her to come, to kill her, or maybe to steal Cara's body. She wouldn't let her.

Cara fled, running past Molly's door and down the steps with the parasol in her hand.

Chapter Ten

"You have such a pretty voice, Mommy." Lindsey looked up at Cara from under the covers during their nightly tuck-in routine. She'd been there for ten days now. She'd been keeping track, wondering what her family thought. Did they think she was dead? They knew she'd never run off with no word to anybody. This had to be so hard on her mom and the rest of the family.

"Thank you, sweetie." Cara had memorized the song by now since she'd been singing it to Lindsey every night. It felt weird knowing she was tucking in such an old entity, this *girl* who never got the chance to grow up, but Lindsey was keeping her and Kyle trapped, threatening their lives.

Cara wiped a few stray hairs off Lindsey's angelic face. At times like these she almost forgot who she was dealing with.

Almost.

What would Lindsey have been like if she'd lived her life? Was she destined to be evil, or was it the years of blaming her innocent sister and guilty father that hardened her heart?

Cara had to escape. Turning a baby over to give Lindsey life wasn't an option.

Ugh. She shouldn't even be considering that there could be a child. She had slept two nights now in bed with Kyle, him on his side, her on hers. He never got too close, and they even used their own blankets, but if they went months of pretending to have sex, Lindsey would question why Cara wasn't getting pregnant. God, what if she demanded to watch them? The thought creeped her out even more.

"Goodnight, sleep tight." Cara gave Lindsey a kiss on the forehead and left the room. She shut the door and started down the hall.

"Come see me," a gentle voice whispered to her, wrapping a soft invisible hand around her arm and leading her to Molly's room.

Cara laid her palm on the door, and warm feelings flowed from her fingertips to her elbow, up the rest of her arm and to her chest.

Lindsey's door flew open with a bang, and Cara jumped.

"What are you doing, Mommy?" Lindsey squealed. "Stay away from Molly's room. She wants to steal you away from me. She'll slit your throat and toss you into the hallway to bleed."

(UN)LUCKY THIRTEEN

"I wasn't doing anything?" Cara didn't know what she had been doing.

Lindsey planted her hands on her hips and stomped her foot. "Do I need to show you what happens?"

"No, I don't want—" The words cut off, and suddenly Cara was standing in the basement staring at a dead body. The pungent aroma of rotting flesh almost made her puke. A thin layer of skin covered the body, pulled tight. Except for the neck where the flesh split apart, a wound created undoubtedly by a sharp knife and a strong swipe.

The crevice seemed to widen, exposing shiny red flesh that hadn't been there before, and a handful of maggots fell to the floor, squirming around. Cara felt like they were suddenly crawling all over her body, and as the metallic smell of blood grew even stronger, she gagged again.

A scream came from one of the other bodies, and then another. Loud painful howls filled the room, but Lindsey didn't even seem to notice.

"Do you see my old mommy? Do you see what happened because she went to Molly's room?" Lindsey shoved Cara, and she stumbled forward. "Is this what you want to happen? Molly hates me, and she will do anything she can to destroy us. She will kill Daddy, and she will kill you."

"I get it. I get it. Can we leave?" Cara begged. The suffering and death of the hellish basement overwhelmed her.

In a flash, they were upstairs, and Lindsey lay down in her bed. She looked up at Cara from under her lashes, and her voice softened. "I don't want to lose you, Mommy."

"I don't want to lose you either." The pressure built in Cara's head, the start of a new headache. She didn't want to die like that other woman, like any of them. "What was that mommy's name?"

All of these women had lives that were taken away, stolen. They had families, possibly even their own children, and they disappeared, trapped in the basement forever.

"It doesn't matter her name. She's gone." Lindsey tugged the blanket up to her chin and closed her eyes.

This was hopeless, absolutely hopeless. There was no way she would get out of the house alive.

Chapter Eleven

Several more days passed, and Cara stood upstairs in the master bedroom staring out the window to the street. Cars drove by, people jogged past, and the whole world kept going even though she was stuck.

"Mommy," Lindsey called, and Cara shuffled out to the top of the steps to find her standing down below. "Daddy and I are making a special project for you in the backyard. So don't come out."

"I won't," Cara said.

There were at least a couple things she appreciated about this world. She didn't have to eat if she didn't want to, and she didn't have to shower because they never sweated and smelled.

It wasn't worth it though.

"Cara," a soft voice called, and she spun around.

Molly.

Cara shot down the hallway past Molly's bedroom and into Lindsey's. Kyle and Lindsey were crossing the yard and disappeared into the trees. Should she go into Molly's room? She didn't want to die, but that feeling was back, tugging on her chest. It was a peaceful feeling, one of hope.

If Molly was so bad, then why did Cara get these warm feelings? Maybe it was her way of fooling her victim.

But death might be preferable to this horrible life. Cara didn't want her soul trapped downstairs with the others. She thought of Kyle—he'd shown her what could happen in the basement, even though he experienced its horrors at Lindsey's hands. He'd risked bringing her down there to show her the truth. She needed to be brave too.

Cara tiptoed down the hall to Molly's room. She might end up with her throat slit like that woman Lindsey showed her, but she had to know about Molly. She cracked the door, peeked in, but saw nobody, so she stepped inside.

The door slipped out of her hand and shut and then locked. The temperature of the room dropped, and Cara tensed. Oh god, she would die in this room; she should have listened to Lindsey. She grappled at the knob, but it slipped in her damp hands

"Cara," the voice said. The girl in the lavender dress and braids sat on the bed. Molly.

Cara's heart raced, and she could hardly breathe. Her neck would be slit like that other woman's. She had to get out before Molly got her, but the damn door still wouldn't open.

"I won't hurt you," Molly said, her voice stronger.

(UN)LUCKY THIRTEEN

She was lying. Molly would kill her, and Cara would bleed out before Kyle and Lindsey found her. "Leave me alone."

"I promise nobody will hurt you here." Molly's silky voice was calm, and a wash of peace settled over Cara. She slowly turned around.

"You killed…" Cara paused. Lindsey hadn't told her the name of the mom with the neck wound.

Molly trudged over to the window. Her long braids fell down the back of her lavender dress as she gazed outside.

"Yes, it's my fault she's dead, but I didn't kill her." Her head drooped, her face not visible anymore, but her sorrowful voice enveloped Cara. "Beatrice tried to help me. Lindsey flew into a rage and sliced her neck open. She would've been trapped here with me except Lindsey brought her to the basement before the life left her."

One of these two girls was lying, and Cara couldn't explain why she trusted Molly over Lindsey, but she did. It was totally believable that Lindsey killed Beatrice for trying to help Molly. Maybe some of the others had died that way too.

"Have you been here since you died?"

Molly's head nodded slowly. "You must know by now how Lindsey lies."

The poor girl had been alone for over a century with nobody to talk to. Molested by her father and murdered by her sister.

Some noises came from the outside, and Molly stared out the window. Even though Cara was still wary, she approached Molly at the window. The girl could've attacked her by now if she'd wanted to.

Kyle was pushing Lindsey on the tire swing, and she squealed when she got high. Cara stayed back in case Lindsey caught sight of her.

"She used to be good. I know she was jealous of me, but something happened that day Papa tried to kill her, and she changed." Molly leaned her palms on the window and peered down on her sister. "She's hurt too many innocent people trying to find life again."

"How do we stop her?" Cara crossed her fingers, hoping Molly would have an answer.

"That's the sad thing. This could've ended a long time ago, but she filled those women's heads with such frightening stories about me that they wouldn't step foot into my bedroom. Every one except Beatrice. And now you." Molly turned her head, her eyes filled with gratitude.

"What do we need to do?"

"Bring her to me. I'm unable to leave, but if you get her in here,"—she paused for a moment—"I can take care of her."

Cara stared into Molly's deep green eyes. Lindsey wasn't afraid of losing Cara or Kyle; the girl was afraid of facing her sister, of them finding out how to get free.

(UN)LUCKY THIRTEEN

Lindsey knew that Molly could stop her, and that was why she always shied away from Molly's room.

"How do I get her in here?"

"You can figure that out."

Cara nodded and stared out the window again. Kyle was galloping around the yard with a laughing Lindsey on his back.

"Maybe I can offer to carry her, and then I'll just step into the room. Do we need to set up a time? I can do it at bedtime."

"It doesn't matter when you do it. I will be ready. I've been ready for decades. As long as she crosses through the doorway and is fully in my room, I can handle her."

Cara didn't ask what that meant, but she didn't care. Lindsey deserved whatever she got.

"Okay then. Tonight."

Cara bit the inside of her lip. She didn't want to hope too much because something might go wrong. Molly might not be able to do what she promised.

Cara needed to plan it all out, so she went downstairs to the parlor to wait, putting all her trust into a dead girl.

Chapter Twelve

"Mommy?"

Something poked Cara in the arm, and she opened her eyes. Lindsey stood next to the chaise lounge, a bouquet of flowers in her hands.

"Look what I got for you," Lindsey thrust the flowers into Cara's face.

She stared at the bouquet of white coneflowers for a moment as her head woke up. She took them from Lindsey and stuck her nose into the bouquet. It smelled heavenly.

"Thank you, sweetie." She ran one of the white petals between two of her fingers.

She had been napping in the parlor. Everything with Molly had been a dream, and she was no closer to freedom than she'd been a few hours ago. Despair started to take hold.

"Daddy was pushing me on the swing. He swung me really high. And then he gave me a piggy back ride." She waved her arm like she was holding a lasso. She'd done that in Cara's dream too.

"That sounds like fun."

Maybe it wasn't a dream, and her conversation with Molly had been real. She thought about it more as Lindsey rambled.

No. She remembered the feelings of peace and hope that Molly had given her.

"Let's go find a vase for these flowers." Cara went to the pantry, and sure enough there was a vase the size she needed.

Kyle was drinking a glass of water at the sink. It's too bad she couldn't trust him with her news; he was too afraid of Molly, and he might rat Cara out to Lindsey. She didn't want to believe he would, but she didn't know him well enough yet.

The whole rest of the day and evening went at a sloth's pace. Cara tried to act normal, but as it got closer to bedtime, she became more on edge. Lindsey might grab the door and keep Cara from pulling her into the room. Or she might scramble away before Molly reached her.

Cara would be good as dead.

"Lindsey, will you do a little piano concert before you go to bed? You play so beautifully, and I'd love to hear some songs."

Lindsey beamed and skipped off to the piano. The music helped calm Cara's nerves and slowed the thoughts flooding her head. She was one hundred percent sure her time with Molly hadn't been a dream, and she had to trust in the girl.

And now it was time.

Cara would either be free, or she'd be stuck in the basement with the other women. Or maybe Lindsey would kill her in Molly's room. At least Molly wouldn't be alone anymore.

"Thank you," Cara finally said, and Lindsey stood and took a silly bow, a grin on her face. "Would you like me to carry you up to your room to tuck you in?"

"Two rides today?" Lindsey looked almost in heaven. The girl who just finished playing some expert level piano piece was excited about getting piggy back rides.

But Cara couldn't forget the evil the little girl had inflicted on so many innocent people. The lives she'd ended, the lives she'd changed. She should've asked Molly what would happen to the women Lindsey had killed. Hopefully they would move on to a better place.

A piggy back might not be good though. Cara needed to hold onto Lindsey with her hands.

"Just a regular ride. So I can get my little girl hugs." It was an odd request since Cara hadn't asked Lindsey for hugs before, but she hopped into Cara's arms.

Cara glanced at the bookshelves, and another idea popped into her head.

"Why don't you pick a book to read." The book would keep Lindsey's hands occupied and make it harder to reach for the doorway. Of course she chose some three-inch thick novel that would undoubtedly be boring. If all went right, it wouldn't matter though.

They trudged up the stairs, Lindsey's blue dress hanging down, and Cara hoped the girl couldn't feel her heart thumping in her chest. She rounded the corner, sending silent thoughts to Molly to get ready. This was her one and only chance, and she didn't want to think about what might happen if it went wrong.

"So what is this book about?" Cara asked. Lindsey babbled about the story as they walked. Her room was down the hall now, Molly's room right before that.

Cara took a few deep breaths. Just a few feet more. She needed to shift Lindsey in her arms but didn't want to distract the rambling girl.

So close… so close…

They reached Molly's room, and Cara quickly stepped to the door and twisted the knob, pushing into the room.

"What are you doing?" Lindsey squealed. Cara had crossed the threshold, but she didn't see Molly. Where was she?

Lindsey tried to escape Cara's grasp, and they both tumbled across the wood floor. The bedroom door slammed, and both stilled. Molly stood in front of the door, her face dark, and her beautiful brown braids hanging like singed rope. Her once bright green eyes were steely gray, and she clenched her fists.

"You've been a bad girl, Lindsey." Molly took a few steps forward, and Cara backed away, her skin clammy.

A roll of thunder roared outside the window, the sky blacker than black. The lights in the room flickered, and Cara tried her hardest not to run.

"No!" Lindsey screamed, and for a moment Cara questioned if she'd done the right thing. Lindsey scrambled behind Cara, clutching at her and jerking Cara's hair. "She'll kill us. What did you do?"

Molly extended her arm, motioning with her finger to come closer.

Oh no, Lindsey was right. Molly was out for revenge, and now Cara would die too.

Lightning flashed outside the window, accompanying the booming thunder. A cold, wet feeling filled Cara's body, and suddenly Lindsey was in front of her. The feeling disappeared. Lindsey flailed around, trying to grasp Cara, but slowly, ever so slowly, she was sliding along the hardwood floor toward Molly. Her feet tried to move, but she stayed on the path for her older sister.

"No, don't. Leave me alone." Lindsey's screams intensified as the wind howled outside. "Help me, Mommy."

Cara crawled backwards on the floor until she hit the wall. Molly continued to draw Lindsey toward her. She clutched at the rug and the dresser but couldn't get a hold of anything.

(UN)LUCKY THIRTEEN

The door flung open, and Kyle gaped at them.

"Daddy, she's going to kill me?" Lindsey yelled. "Help me."

Molly flicked her wrist, and the door slammed again. The heat in the room was as suffocating as Lindsey's screams, which continued until she reached Molly's arms.

"No, no, no!" Lindsey hollered. Molly gathered her little sister up in her arms and held her tight, muting the yelling slightly. She hunched over, keeping Lindsey in her grasp, and they fell in a squirming heap of lavender and blue.

Kyle pounded on the door, and Lindsey's screams echoed in Cara's ears. The lump of fabric writhed on the floor and slowly seemed to melt out of view.

And then the girls were gone.

The storm continued outside, and Kyle swung the door open again and scanned the room. "Where are they?"

"They... they're gone. Molly pulled Lindsey to her, and they just disappeared." Oh god, was she gone for good? Cara scrambled to her feet. "We're still here though."

Rain pelted the windows so hard she thought they might shatter.

"We have to get out of here?" Kyle ran for her and caught her hand. They turned and stepped for the door, but an explosion shook the house.

They looked up as the sound of cracking hit them. The ceiling split apart, revealing the thick dark clouds lit up by the lightning. Rain battered her face, and Cara tried to shield it. They couldn't die now that they were almost free.

"Come on," Kyle said, but before they could move the walls started to crumble. Pieces of the roof crashed around them, and Kyle shoved her out of the way from getting hit.

She stumbled over the debris and fell to the floor. Kyle ran to her and shielded her from the falling light fixture. It sounded like a hundred trains were descending upon the house.

This was it. The end. They were about to die.

Chapter Thirteen

The noise stopped. No more crashes or booms of thunder. Kyle crawled off of Cara.

Matchbox cars littered the carpeted floor, and the bedroom held a twin bed covered with a blue blanket and more cars.

Black shorts and a crumpled pair of white socks lay on the floor.

"Where are we?" Cara asked. She peered out the window into the backyard. Some of the trees that had been in Lindsey's yard were gone, but others still remained. And instead of the tire swing, there was a big playset with swings and a slide.

"I think we're in the other house." Kyle almost seemed in shock.

Footsteps and laughter rang out from behind the door, and Cara froze, but the noise passed by the door and faded.

"How are we going to get out? We can't walk out there. We'll freak them out, and they might call the cops."

Kyle joined her at the window. Cara had been about to put Lindsey to bed, but now the sun was high in the sky.

"Look at this." He pointed down. "They have a back porch too."

All they had to do was crawl out and drop to the grass below.

Kyle unlocked the window, and Cara held her breath.

He pushed, and the window slowly creaked open. He quickly and quietly removed the screen and set it against the wall while Cara slid over a chair from the desk.

"Ladies first." Kyle motioned to her, and she scanned the yard and then crawled up the chair and through the window. Kyle joined her a few moments later. The drop to the ground was a little intimidating, but Kyle went first and promised to catch her.

Cara lay down on her stomach and scooted backwards to the edge. Her legs dropped off, and Kyle grabbed onto her to help lower her down. They stayed still, listening for noise, but heard none.

No fence circled the yard, and Kyle took her hand and led her around the house. Cara tensed up as they hit the edge of the yard, but no wall kept them trapped, and they stepped onto the sidewalk.

She didn't know how much time had passed and if she even had her own apartment to return to, but she was free.

(UN)LUCKY THIRTEEN

Cara stared up at the brown house that now looked so different from the green prison Lindsey had trapped them inside. Twenty-Six Oh Two, Thirteenth Avenue.

It was an address she would never forget.

An address she would never return to.

She said a silent thank you to the young girl who saved her and hoped that Molly and Lindsey were gone for good, and then she looked up into the blue sky.

Freedom never felt so sweet.

Acknowledgments

Thank you to Theresa Paolo for once again helping me out with yet another story. And thanks to my Book Beta Peeps group all the encouragement and for advice about blurbs and such.

Thank you also to any readers out there. I hope you enjoy my stories as much as I enjoy writing them.

About the Author

Reading has always been a big part of Suzi's life. She even won the most-pages-read award a few times in her junior high English class, many years ago. She started several writing projects as a kid but never actually finished anything, and then she took a big break from writing that lasted well into adulthood.

She writes in a variety of genres, including horror, suspense, and women's fiction, and she has even dipped into fantasy slightly with her fairy tale retellings. She also writes young adult novels under the name Suzi Drew.

Her non-writing life includes her family and friends, her sweet and fluffy dog, and an awesome job editing with CookieLynn Publishing. (Oh wait, that's still a part of writing. Seems she can't get away from the written word!)

To find out more about Suzi,
go to www.SuziWieland.com.

Also by Suzi Wieland

<u>Thriller Novels</u>
Black Diamond Dogs

<u>Horror Novels</u>
House of Desire

<u>Horror and Suspense Novellas/Short Stories</u>
Shallow Depths
(Un)lucky Thirteen
Long-Term Effects
The Silent Treatment
A Story to Tell
Panne Dora Pass

Twisted Twins Series
Glenda and Gus
Two for the Price of One
A Hard Split

<u>Fairy Tale Novellas</u>
The Down the Twisted Path Series
The Whole Story
An Unwanted Life
Killing Rosie
The Perfect Meal
When the Forest Cries
In the Queen's Dark Light

Please visit www.SuziWieland.com
for more information.

Milton Keynes UK
Ingram Content Group UK Ltd.
UKHW030844141124
451205UK00004B/225